PUPPY
TALES

BARNES
&NOBLE
BOOKS
NEW YORK

Scholastic Inc.

I LOVE COLORS!

by Hans Wilhelm

Hello Reader! — Level 1

SCHOLASTIC INC.

There are three colors:
RED, YELLOW, and **BLUE**.

I will make a picture.

I can use my tail
as a brush.

Oooops!

This looks good!

I will do some more.

Now I have three colors:
RED, ORANGE,
and YELLOW.

RED mixed with YELLOW makes **ORANGE**.

My feet are still white....

Now they are **BLUE**!

What will happen when
I dip my YELLOW feet
into **BLUE**?

They turn GREEN!
YELLOW mixed with BLUE
makes GREEN.

And now I will dip my
RED tail into **BLUE**.
What will happen?

It turns **PURPLE**!
RED mixed with **BLUE**
makes **PURPLE**.

Uh, oh! The paint is getting sticky and stiff!

Watch out!

Here comes **RAINBOW** Dog!

Splash!!!

Now I'm myself again.

But maybe I should keep
a little bit of color.
What do you think?

I HATE MY BOW!

I HATE MY BOW!

by Hans Wilhelm

Hello Reader! — Level 1

SCHOLASTIC INC.

I hate my bath.

I hate my bow.

I hate my chain.

I hate this baby.

I hate this cat.

Hi, guys. May I play with you?

Oops!

Those guys won't play
with a dog
with a bath
and a bow
and a chain.

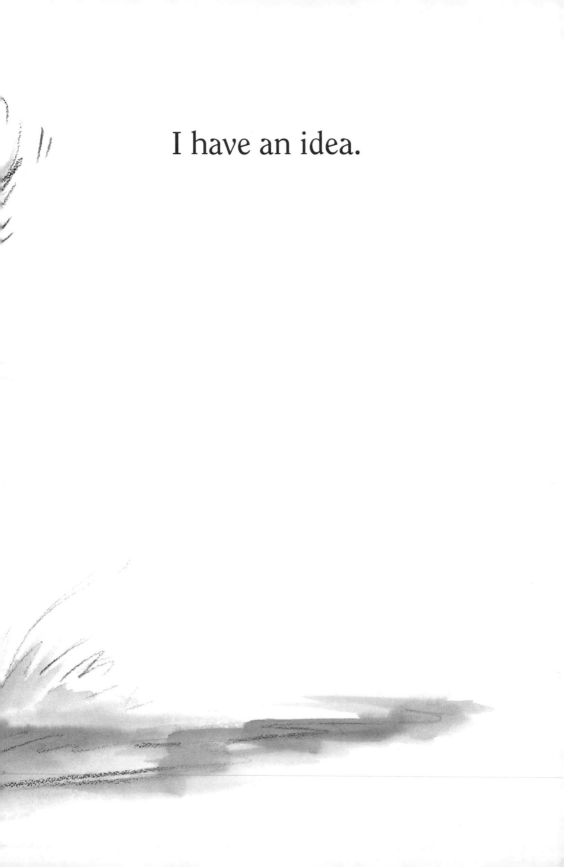

I have an idea.

Come here, cat.

Take the pretty bow.

Come here, baby.

Take the pretty chain.

Now let's play in the mud.

I love my new friends.

I LOST MY TOOTH!

To Sarah
— H.W.

I LOST
MY TOOTH!

by Hans Wilhelm

Hello Reader! — Level 1

SCHOLASTIC INC.

Look, everyone! Look what I have!

I have a loose tooth.

When it falls
out, I will put
it under my
pillow. The
Tooth Fairy
will give
me a treat.

Now I am hungry.

That tastes yummy.

Oh, no!

I lost my tooth!

What will I do?

I have an idea!

There is the camera!

I will take a picture.

Here it comes.

It looks great!

Now the Tooth Fairy will
know all about my tooth.

I hope she comes tonight.

Yes, she was here!
I got my treats!

I wonder which tooth
will be next.

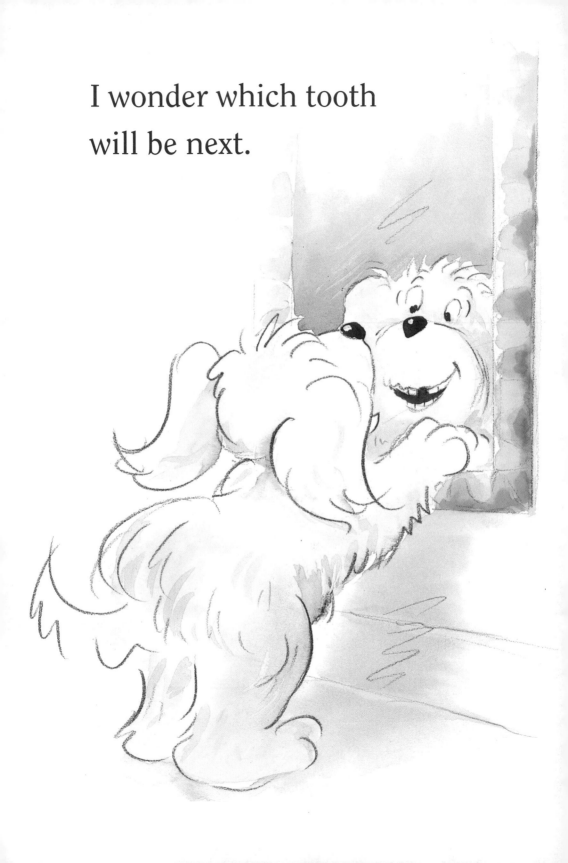

DON'T CUT MY HAIR!

DON'T CUT MY HAIR!

by Hans Wilhelm

Hello Reader! — Level 1

SCHOLASTIC INC.

I don't want a haircut.

I hate this.

I look silly.

Everyone will laugh at me.

I will never go outside again.

My friends are coming to play.
Oh, no!

They must not see me.

What shall I do?

I have an idea!

Hi, guys. Here I come.

How do you like
my cool new look?

My friends like my cool cut.

They wish they had short hair, too.

I like my new haircut.

I AM
LOST!

I AM LOST!

by Hans Wilhelm

Hello Reader! — Level 1

SCHOLASTIC INC.

Oh, what a pretty leaf!

I must catch that leaf.

Come here, leaf.

I got you!

Where am I?

Oh, no! I am lost.

I want to go home.

I need help!

I know what to do.
I'll find a police officer.

Please help me, Officer.

I am lost.

Here is my address.

This is my street.

I am home again.

Thank you, Officer.

IT'S TOO TOO WINDY!

IT'S TOO WINDY!

by Hans Wilhelm

Hello Reader! — Level 1

SCHOLASTIC INC.

I don't want to go outside!

I want to stay inside.

It's too windy.

I hate waiting.

The wind is pulling Baby and me.

The stroller is rolling.
I can't stop it.

Nobody sees us!

What can I do?

I see a street lamp.

I have an idea!

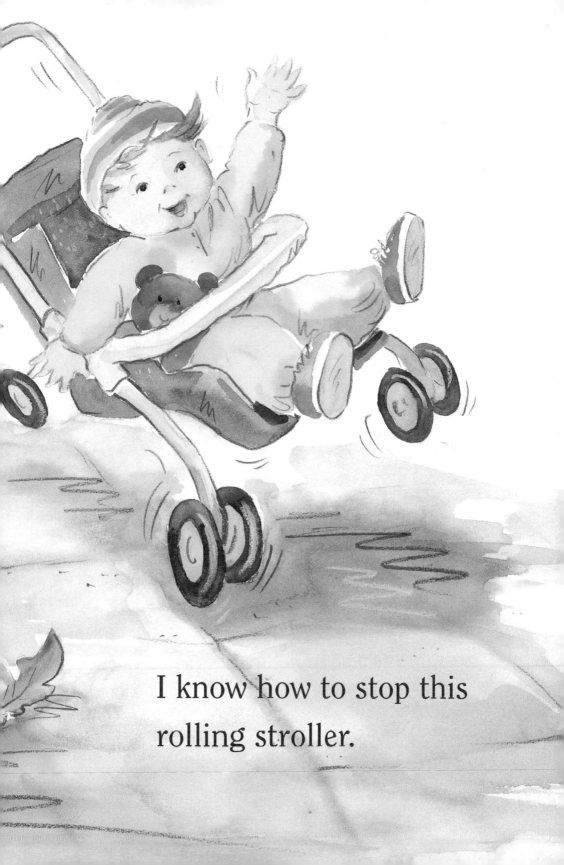

I know how to stop this
rolling stroller.

I did it!
I saved Baby!

Everything is fine!

I deserve a big bone.